This book belongs to

. . . .

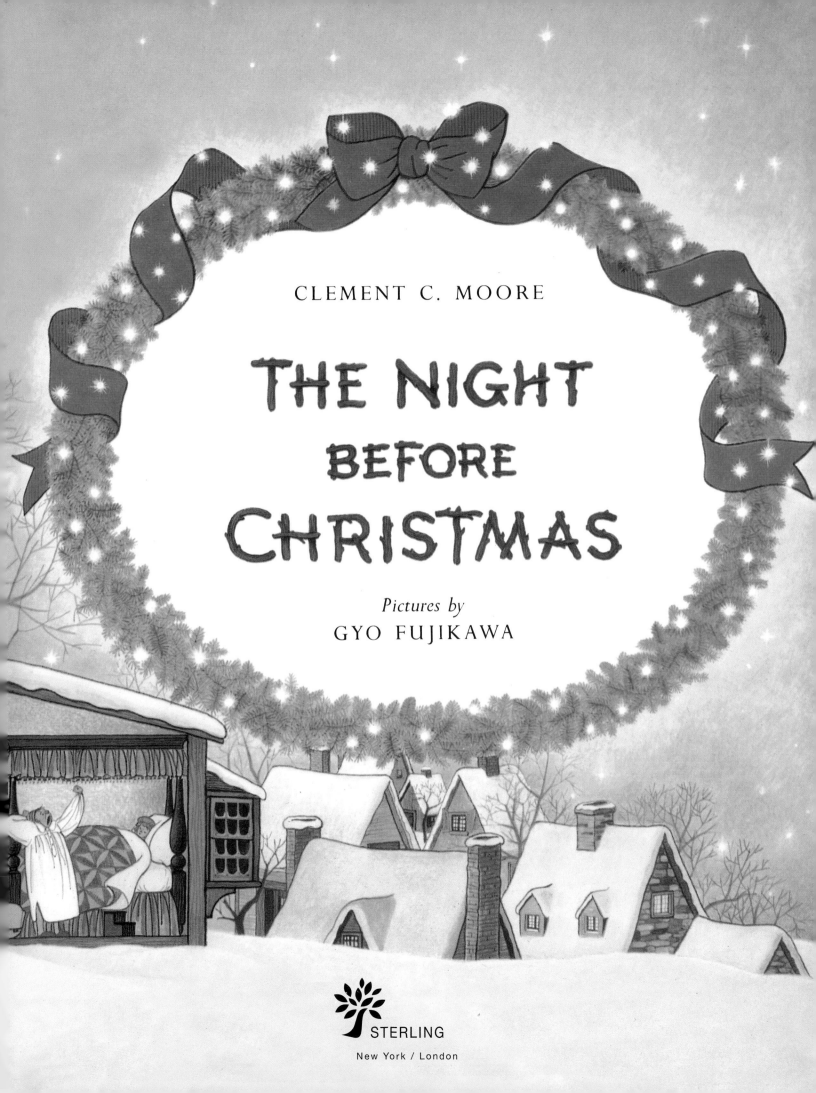

CLEMENT C. MOORE

THE NIGHT BEFORE CHRISTMAS

Pictures by
GYO FUJIKAWA

STERLING

New York / London

STERLING and the distinctive Sterling logo are registered trademarks of
Sterling Publishing Co., Inc.

Library of Congress Cataloging-in-Publication Data

Moore, Clement Clarke, 1779-1863.
Night before Christmas / Clement C. Moore ; illustrated by Gyo Fujikawa.
p. cm.
ISBN-13: 978-1-4027-5065-6
ISBN-10: 1-4027-5065-X
1. Santa Claus—Juvenile poetry. 2. Christmas—Juvenile poetry.
3. Children's poetry, American. I. Fujikawa, Gyo, ill. II. Title.

PS2429.M5N5 2007b
811'.2—dc22

2007008209

2 4 6 8 10 9 7 5 3 1

Published by Sterling Publishing Co., Inc.
387 Park Avenue South, New York, NY 10016
Text © 2007 by Sterling Publishing Co., Inc.
Illustrations © 2007 by The Gyo Fujikawa Copyright Trust
This edition published by Sterling Publishing Co., Inc. by arrangement with
J.B. Communcations, Inc. and Ronald K. Fujikawa.
This book was originally published by Grosset and Dunlap in 1961.
Distributed in Canada by Sterling Publishing
c/o Canadian Manda Group, 165 Dufferin Street
Toronto, Ontario, Canada M6K 3H6
Distributed in the United Kingdom by GMC Distribution Services
Castle Place, 166 High Street, Lewes, East Sussex, England BN7 1XU
Distributed in Australia by Capricorn Link (Australia) Pty. Ltd.
P.O. Box 704, Windsor, NSW 2756, Australia

Printed in China
All rights reserved

Sterling ISBN-13: 978-1-4027-5065-6
ISBN-10: 1-4027-5065-X

For information about custom editions, special sales, premium
and corporate purchases, please contact Sterling Special Sales Department
at 800-805-5489 or specialsales@sterlingpub.com.

'Twas the night before Christmas,
when all through the house
Not a creature was stirring,
not

even

a

mouse;

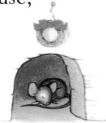

The stockings were hung
by the chimney with care,
In hopes that St. Nicholas
soon would be there;

The children were nestled all snug in their beds,

While visions of sugar-plums danced in their heads;

And Mamma in her 'kerchief,
    and I in my cap,
Had just settled our brains
    for a long winter's nap,

When out on the lawn
    there arose such a clatter,
I sprang from the bed
    to see what was the matter.

Away to the window
    I flew like a flash,
Tore open the shutters
    and threw up the sash.

The moon on the breast
    of the new-fallen snow
Gave the luster of midday
    to objects below,

When,
what to my wondering eyes
    should appear,

But a miniature sleigh,
    and eight tiny reindeer,

With a little old driver,
    so lively and quick,
I knew in a moment
    it must be St. Nick.

More rapid than eagles
his coursers they came,
And he whistled, and shouted,
and called them by name:

"Now, *Dasher!* now, *Dancer!*
   now, *Prancer* and *Vixen!*
On, *Comet!* on, *Cupid!*
   on, *Donder* and *Blitzen!*

To the top of the porch!
   to the top of the wall!
Now dash away! dash away!
   dash away all!''

As dry leaves that before
  the wild hurricane fly,
When they meet with an obstacle,
  mount to the sky,

So up to the housetop
   the coursers they flew,
With the sleigh full of toys,
   and St. Nicholas, too.

And then, in a twinkling,
   I heard on the roof
The prancing and pawing
   of each little hoof.

As I drew in my head,
　　and was turning around,
Down the chimney St. Nicholas
　　came with a bound.

He was dressed all in fur,
　　from his head to his foot,
And his clothes were all tarnished
　　with ashes and soot;

A bundle of toys
　　he had flung on his back,
And he looked like a peddler
　　just opening his pack.

His eyes — how they twinkled!
   his dimples how merry!
His cheeks were like roses,
   his nose like a cherry!

His droll little mouth
      was drawn up like a bow,
And the beard on his chin
      was as white as the snow;

The stump of a pipe
      he held tight in his teeth,
And the smoke it encircled
      his head like a wreath;

He had a broad face
and a little round belly
That shook when he laughed,
like a bowlful of jelly.

He was chubby and plump,
a right jolly old elf,
And I laughed when I saw him,
in spite of myself;

A wink of his eye
and a twist of his head
Soon gave me to know
I had nothing to dread.

He spoke not a word,
    but went straight to his work,
And filled all the stockings;
    then turned with a jerk,

And laying his finger
    aside of his nose,
And giving a nod,
    up the chimney he rose;

He sprang to his sleigh,
    to his team gave a whistle,
And away they all flew
    like the down of a thistle.

But I heard him exclaim,
    ere he drove out of sight,

"Happy Christmas to all and to all a good night."